PALLUQ & QILIQTI
Help Their Anaanatsiaq

WRITTEN BY
Jeela Palluq-Cloutier

ILLUSTRATED BY
Michelle Simpson

One morning, *Palluq** wakes up to the sound of voices in the kitchen. He thinks his parents and brothers must already be up.

Palluq's sister is still sleeping. He wakes her up and goes to get breakfast.

*Palluq (pronounced "PAL-luq"): name

4

After breakfast, Palluq gets ready for school.

"Go and see your *anaanatsiaq** on your way to school," says Palluq's *anaana*.**

Palluq likes helping his anaanatsiaq. He knows it is important to help Elders.

*anaanatsiaq (pronounced "a-NAA-nat-si-aq"): grandmother
**anaana (pronounced "a-NAA-na"): mother

On his way to his anaanatsiaq's house, Palluq runs into his cousin *Qiliqti.** Qiliqti is also on his way to their anaanatsiaq's house.

"Hi, *angutiqatik*,"** says Palluq. "Let's race to Anaanatsiaq's house!" They both start running.

*Qiliqti (pronounced "qil-IQ-ti"): name
**angutiqatik (pronounced "a-ŊU-ti-qa-tik"): kinship name for a cousin through fathers

Qiliqti runs a bit faster than Palluq. He arrives at their anaanatsiaq's house first.

They both *kunik** their anaanatsiaq. Then they look for chores that need to be done.

*kunik (pronounced "KOO-nik"): a kiss given by placing one's nose on a person's face and breathing in

Palluq checks the ice bucket on the porch.
It is almost empty, so he takes it outside
and finds a big chunk of ice. He picks off
small pieces of ice with an ice pick and
places them in the bucket.

Qiliqti shovels the front stairs.

When they are done, they go back inside and ask their anaanatsiaq if she needs any more help.

"Come back after school," says Anaanatsiaq. "The first one here can go to the store and buy flour for me."

The cousins happily walk to school. They are excited to race to their anaanatsiaq's house again after school. Last time Palluq went to the store for his anaanatsiaq she let him use the change to buy a treat.

16

The school day seems really long. When school is finally over, Palluq and Qiliqti run toward their anaanatsiaq's house. They are excited to help their anaanatsiaq again.

This time, Palluq gets to the house first.

Anaanatsiaq gives Palluq money to buy the flour. She says, "Buy whatever you want with the change."

Palluq happily takes the money and says to his cousin, "Let's go to the store together."

Palluq and Qiliqti go to the store to buy flour.

"What should we buy with the change?" asks Qiliqti.

"Let's get some crowberry tea. It is Anaanatsiaq's favourite kind of tea," replies Palluq.

When they get back to Anaanatsiaq's house, they all drink tea together and talk about their day.

Before the cousins leave, Palluq tells Anaanatsiaq that they will come back tomorrow to help her again.

Palluq and Qiliqti love helping their anaanatsiaq!

Inuktitut Glossary

Notes on Inuktitut pronunciation: There are some sounds in Inuktitut that may be unfamiliar to English speakers. The pronunciations below convey those sounds in the following ways:

- A double vowel (for example, *aa*, *ee*) creates a long vowel sound.
- Capitalized letters indicate the emphasis.
- Ŋ is a sound similar to "ng" in the word "sing."
- **q** is a "uvular" sound, which is a sound that comes from the very back of the throat (the uvula). This is different from the **k** sound, which is the same as the typical English **k** sound.

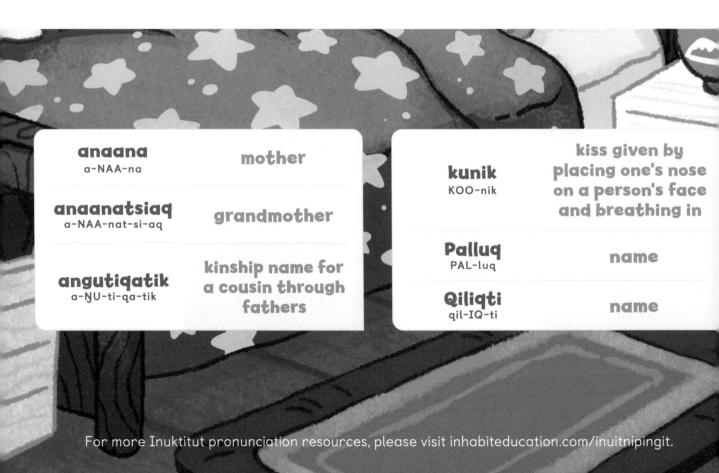

anaana a-NAA-na	mother
anaanatsiaq a-NAA-nat-si-aq	grandmother
angutiqatik a-ŊU-ti-qa-tik	kinship name for a cousin through fathers

kunik KOO-nik	kiss given by placing one's nose on a person's face and breathing in
Palluq PAL-luq	name
Qiliqti qil-IQ-ti	name